THE LITTLE PRINCE

ONCE UPON A TIME, THERE WAS
A BOY NAMED LITTLE PRINCE.
HE LIVED ON ASTEROID B-612,
A VERY TINY PLANET.

THE LITTLE PRINCE HAD MANY TASKS ON HIS PLANET. ONE OF THEM WAS TO MAKE SURE THE BAOBAB TREES DIDN'T GROW AND TAKE OVER EVERYTHING!

ONE DAY, THE WIND BROUGHT A FLOWER
SEED, WHICH QUICKLY SPROUTED
AND GREW.

THE FLOWER TURNED INTO A BEAUTIFUL ROSE, AND THE LITTLE PRINCE BEGAN TO TAKE CARE OF HER EVERY DAY. TO PROTECT HER, HE COVERED HER WITH A GLASS DOME.

THE LITTLE PRINCE AND THE ROSE WERE ALWAYS TOGETHER. THEY LOVED LOOKING AT THE STARS AND ALWAYS KEPT EACH OTHER COMPANY.

HOWEVER, ONE DAY, THE LITTLE BOY DECIDED
TO SET OFF FOR NEW ADVENTURES.

HE TOOK ADVANTAGE OF
A MIGRATION OF BIRDS TO
EXPLORE NEW PLACES AND
MAKE NEW FRIENDS.

AS HE WAS IN AN ASTEROID ZONE, HE
WANTED TO GO VISIT THEM.

THE FIRST ASTEROID HOUSED A SOLITARY
KING WHO LOVED TO GIVE ORDERS.

AUTHORITARIAN, THE MAN WANTED THE LITTLE PRINCE TO BE HIS SUBJECT. BUT THE LITTLE BOY DIDN'T LIKE THE IDEA AND SOON DEPARTED FOR ANOTHER ASTEROID.

ON THE SECOND ASTEROID LIVED A VERY VAIN MAN WHO LIKED TO RECEIVE COMPLIMENTS AND APPLAUSE ALL THE TIME.

THE LITTLE PRINCE FOUND THAT BEHAVIOR
VERY STRANGE AND CONTINUED HIS JOURNEY.

ON THE THIRD ASTEROID LIVED A LAMPLIGHTER
WHO DID NOTHING BUT OBEY ORDERS.

THE LITTLE BOY FOUND THAT TASK VERY DULL, AND ONCE AGAIN, HE DEPARTED.

SO, THE LITTLE PRINCE ARRIVED ON PLANET
EARTH, WHERE HE FOUND A FOX.

THE BOY TOLD THE ANIMAL THAT HE WANTED TO MAKE FRIENDS, AND THE FOX REPLIED THAT, IN ORDER TO DO SO, HE MUST TAME HER.

OVER TIME, THE FOX AND THE LITTLE PRINCE
BECAME GREAT FRIENDS.

IN THIS WAY, THE BOY DISCOVERED THAT THE ROSE WAS ALSO HIS FRIEND AND THAT HE MISSED HER VERY MUCH. THEREFORE, HE DECIDED TO RETURN TO HIS PLANET, WHICH LEFT THE FOX SAD.

THE LITTLE PRINCE REALIZED THAT HE WOULD
ALSO MISS THE FOX, SO HE DECIDED TO TAKE
HER TO ASTEROID B-612.

UPON ARRIVING THERE, THE LITTLE PRINCE WAS
VERY HAPPY TO SEE HIS BELOVED FLOWER AGAIN,
BUT HE NEVER FORGOT THE FRIENDSHIPS HE
HAD MADE ON PLANET EARTH.

THE END